This book belongs to

....

....

This format first published in the United States 2005
by Grosset & Dunlap
A division of Penguin Young Readers Group
345 Hudson Street, New York, New York 10014
Original edition first published in Great Britain 2004
by Frederick Warne & Co
Copyright © Eric Hill, 2004
All rights reserved
Planned and produced by Ventura Publishing Ltd.
80 Strand, London WC2R 0RL, England
Printed in Singapore
ISBN 0-448-43811-9
1 3 5 7 9 10 8 6 4 2

Spot's
Show-and-Tell

Eric Hill

Grosset & Dunlap • New York

Spot and his friends arrived at school bright and early

"Hello, everyone," said Miss Bear.

When everyone was settled, Miss Bear asked, "Does anyone have anything special for show-and-tell today?"

Helen and Tom both
put their hands up.

Miss Bear asked Helen to come up first. Helen held up her pink ballet shoes for everyone to see. They had lovely ribbons to keep them on her feet.

"Every week I go to ballet class," said Helen. "Next week we're giving a recital and I'm going to be a flower!"

Everyone thought Helen's ballet shoes were very special. They all clapped. Helen was very happy.

Next it was Tom's turn. "I've brought my new kite," said Tom. "It's very special. My dad helped me to make it. We used special paper, wooden sticks, and glue. We're going to fly it on Saturday."

Everyone thought Tom's kite was wonderful and they all clapped. Tom was very happy.

Later that morning, it was time for painting.
Spot and Steve shared an easel.

"I'm going to bring something
for show-and-tell tomorrow," said Spot.

"Me too," said Steve. "But I'm not sure what to bring."

"Neither am I," said Spot. "We'll have to think hard, won't we?"

That afternoon, Steve was going to Spot's house to play. Sally picked Spot and Steve up and they all walked home together.

Steve saw a bright orange leaf on the grass and he picked it up. "Maybe I'll take this for show-and-tell tomorrow," he said. "It's a lovely color!"

When they got back, Spot and Steve played cars in Spot's room.

"My car collection is special," Spot said to Steve.
"Maybe I'll take my cars to show-and-tell tomorrow."
"That's a good idea," said Steve.

At bedtime, Spot was still thinking about show-and-tell. Suddenly, he had a great idea. "I know what I want to take to show-and-tell tomorrow," Spot told his mom. "It's very, very special."

"That sounds perfect!" said Sally, and she kissed
Spot goodnight. "Sweet dreams, Spot!"

The next morning, Spot was smiling and cheerful when he met Steve on the way to school.
"Have you got something for show-and-tell?" asked Steve.
"Yes," said Spot. "And it's very, very special. Have you got something?"
"Yes," said Steve happily.
"And it's very special too."

At school, Miss Bear asked who had brought in something for show-and-tell.

Spot and Steve put their hands up and Miss Bear asked them to come to the front of the class.

"I'd like to show the picture I painted of my friend Spot!" said Steve.

Spot laughed. "And I'd like to show the picture I painted of my friend Steve," said Spot.

Everyone clapped, even Miss Bear! Spot and Steve were very, very happy!